# TWIN CITIES

# Also by Jose Pimienta

*Suncatcher*

*Stars, Hide Your Fire* (with Kel McDonald)

*Soupy Leaves Home* (with Cecil Castellucci)

# TWIN CITIES

JOSE PIMIENTA

NEW YORK

**_Twin Cities_ was penciled and inked traditionally, and colored and lettered in Photoshop.**



Visit us on the web! RHKidsGraphic.com • @RHKidsGraphic

Educators and librarians, for a variety of teaching tools, visit us at RHTeachersLibrarians.com

Library of Congress Cataloging-in-Publication Data is available upon request.
ISBN 978-0-593-18063-1 (hardcover) — ISBN 978-0-593-18062-4 (paperback)
ISBN 978-0-593-18064-8 (lib. bdg.) — ISBN 978-0-593-18065-5 (ebook)

Designed by Patrick Crotty

MANUFACTURED IN CHINA
10 9 8 7 6 5 4 3 2 1
First Edition

A comic on every bookshelf.

To my siblings. I love you.

Mexicali, Mexico.
HOTEL DEL NORTE HOTEL

FARMACIAS
De los Santos
BEBIDAS
El Rosario
DANA LIN

GRANDON
CINE
2X1

Musical Chavez
Boutique Géminis
HERMAN

TEATRO DEL ESTADO

EL PODER DEL SER

XOXO

Yes!
Vacation time!
Finally!
Yeah!
Woo-hoo!
We did it!
DIPLOMA

Picture time, Lu-lu Twin!
Fernando, please call me Teresa.

We graduated sixth grade!
What a lovely ceremony!
Let's take a group photo.
Fernando, give your camera to my mom.

Do you have summer plans, Lu-lus?
Yes!

Get together. This is the good one.
One, two, three.
SMILE!

It's official. Sixth grade is over.

Ready to go, Lu-lus?
MOM!

Oh, right— I am sorry, Teresa.

CALEXICO

I'm excited to see how these come out.

Okay, kids. Be on your best behavior. Remember to only speak if they ask you something.
AYUDA

Honey, their passports?

Where are you headed today?
Just here, to Calexico, sir. We're celebrating a graduation.

6

FroZone
Menu

Kids, this year we're going to skip going to Rosarito for the summer.
You're going to help Mom and me at our office and around the house.

Is it because you're spending so much on Teresa's new bedroom?
Wow, thanks, Fer.

It's not that. We want you to have more responsibilities.

Also, you'll help me with the yard.

But we don't like gardening.
I like it okay—

I'm not interested in whether you like it or not.
You're going to help me.
AUTO

I wish I got the yard work.

So, Teresa, you're gonna be seeing this place on a daily basis by August.
USA GAS
MEGA
WILL WHITE

I'm so happy about it! I'm excited that they start school so early.

Fer, are you still glad you chose to stay in Mexicali?

My friends will be there.

Stick with who you know, right?

Mom, I'm getting full. I don't think I can eat any more.

Teresa, you barely ate any of it.

I thought it'd be smaller.
Typical—always backing out of things.

I'm not backing out. I'm full.

Okay, you two. That's enough.

I'll have some of it.
Gordo, do you want some?

Ready to go home, kids?
We're getting produce here in Calexico, right?
Yes.
SUN POP
bear

open late.

Let's go, Lu-lu!

It's Teresa.

MEXICO
NADA QUE DECLARAR
NADA QUE DECLARAR
NADA QUE DECLARAR
DEL NORTE

Gosh, it's hot.
And it's only June.
Do you think they'll turn on the AC later?
Nah. It's not even ninety today.
It's not even thirty-two Celsius?
I'm going to need your help in a minute, kids.
Okay!
Sure!
Under Construction

Under Construction

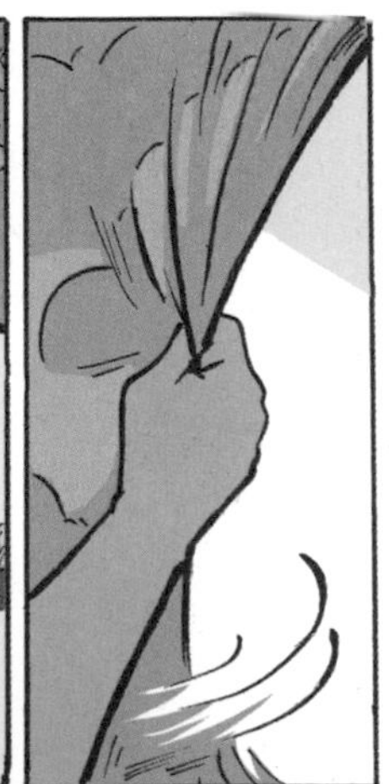

Don't worry. Your new room will be ready soon.

Dad says delays are normal.

Did you believe Mom about why we're not going to Rosarito?

Well, Mom doesn't lie to us.

But she doesn't tell us everything. Like how much my new school will cost.

Rosarito is fun, but maybe it's time we do something different.

Mmm. I guess.

Diccionario
The Universe
EL CANTO
Centinela
FRONTERA
Imperial
EADG
Postlethwaite

RASPADOS
NATURALES

RAMIRES

You're sure you're happy with staying in Mexicali for seventh grade?
This question again? Yes!

Who wants to be crossing the border every day to go to school?

You're weirded out by anything different.

That's not true.

Plus—once I'm in an American middle school, high school will be easier to get in to.

And after that, American college.
We're twelve, Teresa. Can we just focus on that?

ER
CTION

Good morning, dear.
Good morning, Mom.

Isn't it a great coincidence that we both start school the same day?
Yes!

Could you be any MORE gross?
Probably! Do we have any mayo?

Ugh—I'm SO glad we're not having lunch together anymore.

BEEPP BEEPP

That's my car pool!
Aw, we're not brushing our teeth together?
FRONTIER

What about the funny faces?

I need to be ready earlier from now on. Crossing the border, remember?

MUAH!

Okay, okay, Mom! Bye!

Alright, Fernando. You'd better start getting ready. I'll prepare your lunch.
Ketc

Can I have some corn chips with my lunch?

I don't like you eating junk food for lunch.

You can have some after dinner tonight.

TEN

Please pass it forward.

I wonder where Tony and Victor are.

Ugh. All these desks are right-handed.

Stop looking at your watch, Fernando.

HOLY
ACAD

Hi, Caro!
WELCOME
EVERYON

PIZZA $1
Hot Dog $1
Tacos $1
MENU

Tell Fer we say hello!
You got it, Tony!

So take good notes, kids.

RRIIINNGG

COLEGIO DE LA CRUZ

I'm home!

RIIINNG

NADA QUE DECLARAR
NADA QUE DECLARAR

Dr. Vilchis
ARGENTINA
FARMACIA VERA 2000
DAVID
TAXI

Hey, you!
Hey, you! How was it?

They have pizza available for lunch! And we get two recesses!

We have different teachers for each subject.

Remember how we only had one teacher all day? Middle school is so different.

Yeah, they do that too on the other side.

Oh, yeah, I saw Tony and Victor during lunch. They got so tall over the summer.

What? I didn't know they were going to your school! I was looking for them today.

What do you mean? Of course you knew. They talked about it several times before.

I don't remember that.

You mean you weren't paying attention.

Maybe they didn't say it loud enough.

Well, who did you eat lunch with at recess?

I didn't eat anything. I...played soccer.

You must have been hungry when you got home.

Nah—I was waiting for us to eat together.
Oh, you don't have to do that. Who knows how long it will take me to cross back.

Food is ready, you two.

RACE YA!!

CITY OF CA
JMP
VIVAI
CUCAPA
COLUNC

I'm getting a lot of homework for my first week.

Mmm...

78
I love PE!

Are you lost?

I asked if you're lost.

Um...no. I'm just...I was...

Do you want to sit down for a bit?

Oh. Eh—no, thank you. I don't—

Come sit.

Would you like a corn chip?
Sure!
PAPAS CHEMA

Wow, take the whole bag while you're at it.
PAPAS CHEMA

I'm sorry. I didn't mean to—
It's okay. I'm teasing. I offered.

Thanks. I don't get to eat them too often.
Well, they sell them here at our snack store. Is this your first year?

I used to go to elementary school here. But middle school is a lot different.

I know. It sucks, right?

Yes. A lot. It's the worst place ever.
Haha. Okay, maybe not the worst place ever. But pretty bad.

This is also my first year here.
What grade are you in?

Take a guess!

Third of middle school?
Well, there's only three years of middle school, so I guess it's not a hard guess.

But you got it wrong. I'm in second year.

Oh.

So, seriously, what are you doing back here?

I was looking for a place to eat my lunch.

Right, but you're empty-handed.
Je-je. Okay, sure. Hmm. Well, I come out here during recess to eat my lunch.
I meant for tomorrow.
Oh.

Make sure teachers don't see you. We're not allowed to be back here.
PAPAS CHEMA

Do you want the last ones?
PAPAS CHEMA

Science &
1.- Who were Romulos
2.- Where
3.- Examples
4.- Byzantin
5.- Roman

Pocket sized dictionary
English-Spanish
E S
English-Spanish

CA

Science & Purity!
1- Who were Romulus and Remus?
Teresa?
Can you tell me an
example of Roman
technology?

Ehm...Sister
Martha, what's the
English word for
"acueductos"?

Aqueducts.

Oh, cool!
Okay, then.
Aqueducts.

Thank you,
Teresa.

That was really cool to ask Sister Martha what that word meant. I would have been embarrassed.
Yeah, seriously. I would have just said, "I don't know."
I would have said, "Sorry, no speak-o inglés."

HAHAHAHAHAHAHA
JAJAJAJA
JAJAJAJAJAJAJAJA
HAHAHAHA HI

I was nervous. The vocabulary is more advanced than I thought.

Yeah, but you speak fluent Spanish, too. I struggle with that a lot.
You don't speak Spanish at home?
My mom speaks it to me, but I don't use it much.

Me neither. I understand it, and I can read it, but it's very confusing.

If it wasn't for after-school English classes, I would struggle more.
PIZZA

You go to
after-school
classes?

Yeah. It was
between that
and karate.
Eh—karate in
a heartbeat.

I went to a
class and the sensei
was a jerk.
Eh—English in
a heartbeat.

What do you
do after school,
Teresa?
Mostly homework
or watch TV with
my brother.

You mean
your twin?

Well, yes.
Ugh, I mean, no...
but...mmm...
What?

I'm sorry, did I say something wrong?
No. Yes. Umm...

Yes, I watch TV with my twin brother.

Does anyone wanna play squares?
YES!

TIA OLGA
Don't spoil your appetite.

Your sister will be home soon.

FroZone

International Border
Mexicali
CASA DE CAMBIO
TAX & DUTY FREE

School was kinda boring today. But I met a cool guy.
His name is Alex.
Yeah?

Yeah, and our physics teacher told us a really funny joke in the middle of dictation.
Uh-huh.
click

Do you want to hear the joke?

Can it wait a little bit?

It's really funny.

Okay, I'll just tell you. So, a man sitting cross-legged is watching a tennis match. And he's watching the ball go back and forth—
Fernando! I have to read this for class tomorrow.

EEEEEEAA

Seriously? Please, I have to concentrate.

Did you say turn it up? Sure.
WHAT IS WRONG WITH YOU? TURN IT OFF!

Kids, stop yelling! It's almost time to eat.

Mom! Fer is not letting me do homework.
Don't yell at me, Teresa.

Fer, come help me set the table.

Hey. Are you lost again?
DISC

Not today.
What are you listening to?
DISC

They're a band called La Lupita.

JA-JA-JA
What a great drumbeat.
DISC

1/2
the question.
TAP
TAP
TAP
TAP
(b)Mac
(c)Dill
(d)Boo
In your own
THE BEST READING LIST
COMICS ARE LIT!

I can't believe you haven't heard this band before.
They're one of the most popular bands in all of Mexico.
I mean, it's no Pearl Jam, but—
Pff. Gimme that—
This is way better than those noisy gringos.
(a)
(b)
(c)
(d)
That's a fact.

2/2
10: Write an essay on chapter three.
Good luck!
PKSHH
JE-JE-JE
Shhh
I got this.

Not now, Fernando!

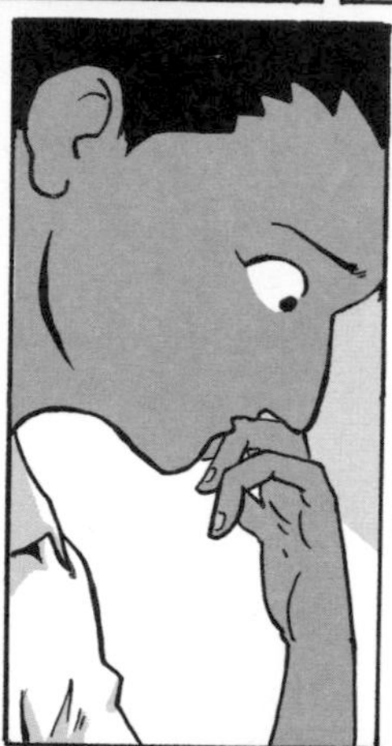

YOU ARE IMPOSSIBLE!
I'M IN MY ROOM!

SWOOSH

DAN

-Sorry-
I'm sorry-
It's okay-I'm
Not- I' Knoin'

Under Construction

SLAAM!!!!

Tia
VANGE
1960
B.C.
ABARROTES
CERVEZA
1099

Feuchter
tel. 568-11-09
Boutique
MATH

DIOS
AYUD

SODA
AGUA

WHAT?

But I studied so hard!
This has never happened.
Science & Purity
English
50%

Well, you did a little less than okay on the first part.
And in the last part, you didn't really write an essay.

But I answered what was in the textbook. I memorized it all.

Yes, but that's not an essay.

I was asking what you thought. Memorizing is not the same as analyzing.
2/2
10. Write an essay on chapter three.

Sister Irma?
My mom will kill me if she sees this grade. How can I make it better?

Well, first, take it easy. It was just a practice quiz.
Write or Draw

Maybe you should read more essays to help you understand their structure.
Is there a book called "Good Essays" I can have?

I'm sure such a book exists, but—come with me.
COMICS

Let's see now—oh, here's something.

SOIAREADS
So you think you're a smart writer?
BE WRITER-ER
Gloria Martinez
Martinez-So you think

This contains the difference between a story, a report, and an essay.
Plus, she's very funny.

She has an essay about why she thinks Mexicali shouldn't have been the capital of the state.
Is she from Mexicali?

Well, that's a long story, but—

Why don't you borrow this and see if it helps you?

I can take this home?

Well, I don't want you missing your recess.
Speaking of which, go play. I'll leave this on your desk.

Thank you. Okay, bye!

Where were you?
I was talking to Sister Irma.

I am SO tired. Waking up extra early is harder than I thought.

What time do you get up?
At about five fifteen.

Ugh—why?

I get up around that time. Sometimes a little earlier.
Again, why?

Well, I have to get ready and we only have one bathroom.

And don't you carpool? So you have to pick up a lot of other kids.

You don't carpool, Caro?
Nah. My dad drives me everyday since he works on this side.

I mean, but you also get extra time to do homework, right?
I'd take the extra time to sleep any day.

In a heartbeat.

TOTALLY
DUDE
Hee
Hee
Hee
Hee
Yeah
PIZZ

UGGH

WE ALL KNOW WHAT YOU'RE DOING!

We do?

Ugh, they're in eighth grade and they go behind the gym thinking we can't smell them.

They smell like my aunt's cigarettes.
I don't think those boys were smoking cigarettes, Maggie.

And neither is your aunt, if that's what they smell like.

That smell is so strong. Don't they get caught?

I don't know. But they've been doing it since the sixth grade.

Maybe the school doesn't want to get them in trouble.
Wait. What are they smoking?

Weed, Maggie! They're smoking weed!
Isn't that illegal?
PIZZ

Alex told me this great joke.
So Pepito is at school and his teacher asks, "Pepito, what's faster?
"A lighting bolt or the light switch?"
And Pepito says, "Diarrhea, Miss.
Papelería La Abeja
KDM

"Because the other day, I ran like a lightning bolt—
ESTADIO
MXL
2000

"and turned on the light, but it was too late."
UABC

FERNANDO! That's gross!
Tel. 5-54-60-06

OXXO

Is your school getting any better?

Yeah, I think it's—

Wait, when did it have to get better?

I dunno. My school's not great. I figured yours must be the same.

No, I'm having a good time. Nadia is very funny and Maggie is super sweet.

There's also this one kid, Ed, who is always using his pens as drumsticks and asking me to guess the song.

Does he live around here? We'd be a good team at that game.

No, he lives in Calexico.

Oh.

Tony and Victor say hi, by the way. I still can't believe you forgot they were going to school with me.

We weren't THAT close.

Recess is the best part of the school day. Sometimes Alex brings his CD player and we listen to music.

Are those allowed in school?

He doesn't care. And he always gives me corn chips at lunch.

Mom doesn't like you eating that at lunch.

MMDssnt mememememeh—
SEP
Matemáticas

You're not gonna tell, right?

KIDS!
We're going out to eat, so get ready.
Where are we going?
The Dragon Mission. It's close by, so—

YES!

Whoa there, missy.

What?

Come here really quick.

You had quite a growth spurt.

Fernando, come over here. I wanna compare you both.

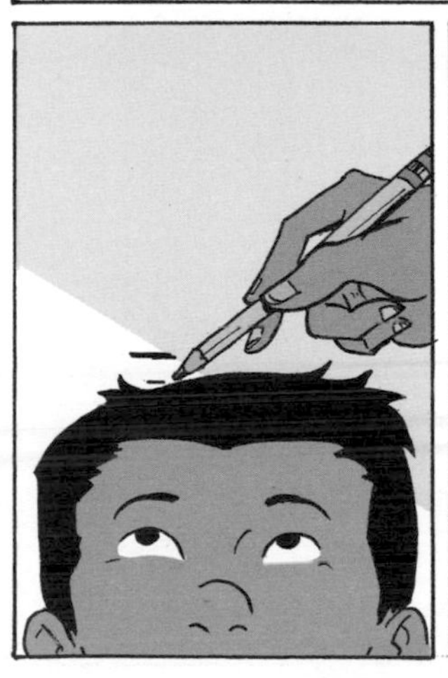

You're not THAT much taller.

Do you want more fried rice, Fer?
Yes, please.

So, kids, we want to talk to you about your upcoming birthday.
CERVEZA

Do we have to do something for the both of us?

It will make it much easier to coordinate, honey.

But we can do whatever you two want to do.
We can go to a quermés or we can drive to the Guadalupe Canyon for a day trip.

Can we go on a day trip to San Diego?
That may be a bit too far of a drive for a day trip.
Fer, do you have anything in mind?
We could go to Mundo Divertido.
We like it there, right, Teresa?
Mmm...we've been there a lot.
Then how about a trip to the zoo?
For a birthday?
FINE! YOU suggest something and I'll tell you it's boring.
Fernando!

Okay. How about we go to the movies with friends?
Nah—well— maybe—
SALIDA

That could work. I could drive you and some of your friends to the Cinépolis.

Well, I was hoping we could go to the movies in Imperial.
CERVEZA
Imperial, California?

Hmm...I suppose we can make a day out of it.
After the movie, we could go to that buffet place.

As long as it's only a couple of friends, I guess that's okay.

Yeah! I like that plan.
Fer, did you eat the last carnitas?
No.

YES YOU DID! WHY? I BARE—
Okay, calm down, Teresa. Look, there's still chicken here—

It's NOT the same.

Fer, give your sister some of yours.
She never finishes what's on her plate! Why do—

I didn't ask you, Fernando.

Joven. La cuenta, por favor.

La Misión Dragón

You're going to dig a lot of the stuff in here. There are some excellent South American bands, too.
PA' LA RAZA
CD-R

Oh, awesome! But I can't listen to this.
Does your mom not let you?

No, it's not that. It's just that...I don't have a CD player.

Oh, pff—well, that's a simple fix. I can turn this into a tape.

You don't have to—
Hey, don't sweat it.

Helps me to make sure I'm giving you good stuff.

Or you can come over to my place and listen to it there.
And if there's a song you're not into—poof! Gone from the mix.
Cool.

So I was wondering if you'd like to come to my birthday thing. My birthday is on the thirteenth, but we're celebrating it the day after.

Nice! Are you having a party?
No. We're actually going to the movie theater in Imperial.

On the other side?
Yeah.

Sorry—
I can't make that happen.

Oh. Why?

I don't cross the border. But I'll get you something.

Hey, how about this? Wanna come to a quinceañera with me this weekend?
DEFINITELY! How did you get invited?

Don't be fooled. Minus the occasional fistfight, I'm actually pretty sociable.

I mean, obviously.

Ja-ja. Well, they don't go to this school. But yeah, I have some friends in high school.

TAP!

Cool.

And if you come with me, you can help me out with some stuff.
With what?

Ah—don't worry about it. It's all cool.
Okay. I'll ask my parents about going.

So you never go to Calexico?
Nope.

Not even to the FroZone?
Pff— we have La Michoacana.
ACACIA

Absolutely not.
But, MOM! I got invited!

You're twelve years old.

I'm ALMOST thirteen.
And a quinceañera is no place for a thirteen-year-old.
That's not true!
It is true.

What's true?
Short day for you, too, honey?

Tell her it's not true, Dad!
Stop it, Luis Fernando.

How was your day, dear?
Tell her I'm not too young.

Fer, drop it!
Have you been here awhile?
No.
No what?
La Resolana
La Resolana
La Resolana
Fer, enough!
What?
What is going on?

She—
'Perate, tú! My clients came in earlier and that freed my afternoon.

So I picked up Fernando from school and he got invited to a quinceañera and our answer is no.

Our answer?
You are not going.

I see.

Well?

Hi, Fer.
Our parents are terrible and we should run away.

Okay, well, I'm gonna get my homework started.

Ugh—you always side with them.

Under Constr_tion

Hey. How about a quick race?

Yeah, okay.

Seriously, where would you go if you ran away?
I dunno. We could go to a friend's house. Or Grandma's.

I think those would be the first places they'd look.
Okay, let's think of other places.

Turn that off if you haven't finished your homework.

Yes, Mom.

RRR—I can't do ANYTHING in this house.

GARCIA
10

AQUI
CD's
CASSETTES!
VINILES!!
HISTERIA
Chiri
CHEL
LEY

DANI
BAILA!

LMD-2013

Matilda
Matilda

B#
Librería
YAQUI

Dulceria Lourdes

DISEÑOS
TAGACCI

OSIRIS

ESCUENTO
Y MAS
UABC

Aww!
These look
awesome!
Yeah, it
was a good
party.

Also,
here.
My offer
to come over
still stands,
though.
PA'LA RAZA

We can
just hang and
watch Telehit.
Is that
like MTV?

Yeah, but
they play more
Latino music and no
reality TV shows.

So who
took these
pictures?
I did. I got
them developed
yesterday.

You're
good.

Je-je. Thanks. Do you take photos as well?
Yeah, I try.

I'm working on a big collage.

No way! Like cutting photos and making a big piece?
YEAH!

That's cool. I don't do much with mine, but I just like taking photos.

When can you come over?
Hopefully, soon.

RIINNGG
Aww—recess is over?
Ugh—I have PE next.

C'mon in. Get comfortable.
Wow! You have a TV in your room?

Yeah—what if I wanna watch something my parents don't?

You don't have any siblings?

Not here, no.
Where are they?

They all live on the other side. They're, like, way older than me, so—

SODA ESTEREO
MARIACHI

Do you have other books like this, Sister?
Oh. Did you finish this book?
I read some of it. But I couldn't finish it.
Hmm. Why don't you check out our library after classes today?
I can't go after school. I have to catch my car pool.
Oh, I see. Well, would you consider joining an after-school club?
Some parents volunteer to drive students back to Mexicali.
There's some good choices and it could help.
Hmm. I can talk to my mom about this—
SIGN UP!
Name:
Grade:
Club:

That was such a good video.

Sure was.
So I wanna ask you something, but I need to know if you're cool.
Of course I'm cool. I do cool things.

No, I mean... I wanna know if I offer you something, you're gonna be cool.

Of course I will. Because I'm totally cool.

Do you know what I'm asking?

Oh yeah.

Ugh—more words I don't understand.
Under Constru
Hey, Teresa. Want to come with me on some errands?
Oh, hi, Dad. Ehm. Well, I have some homework to get to.
Oh, that's okay. We won't be long.

Are you cool with a little secret?

Doesn't that stuff... stunt your growth?

Ja-ja- where did you hear that?
I dunno— every expert?

No, it doesn't. It just relaxes you and makes whatever it is you're watching a bit more fun.
Mmm... I dunno. I'm going home soon.

Don't worry. I do this in here all the time.

If your eyes turn red, I have eye drops.
Mmm...
What? C'mon. Don't let me do this alone.

So...school is good?
11
It's hard.

Well, that's why you try harder.

And I like it a lot, but getting up so early is tough.
OFERTA
20¢

You just have to go to bed earlier, then.
13
I try, but I want to double-check my homework and get in some reading.

But if you make sure you're efficient with your time—

it shouldn't be a worry.
Just make the time for it.

3 B's!
BUENO, BONITO, BARATO!!

Look, we can start small.
Just a small puff.
PLAZA de TOROS
You watch too many movies.
Minas de SINALOA
Try it.

Pepino
Camote
$40/kg
Arroz Salvaje
30 HUEVOS BLANCOS SELECCIONADOS
HUEVO BLANCO $35
NANA
Chocolate 39
BARRA
Verduras
Aguacate
GRAN SELECCION
$23/
CHE
LENGUA DE RES
CARNE MOLIDA
kg
22
MARU
DAVID
DELICIAS
JOSS

My stomach hurts.
C'mon. Snacks will fix that.
You have a lot of Mexican snacks.
They're the best—
Pulpos
Churro
Mamut
Most of them are spicy but, like, tangy?
Pff—you mean flavorful. Here—have some.
I can't believe you don't cross the border. Like—there're movies over there.
You wanna see good movies? I gotcha—

Teresa? Can you come over and help me with the laundry?
I'm super busy, Mom!

Oh, okay. Teresa? Come here and help me with the laundry.
Mom! I have—

NOW, Luisa Teresa Sosa! Don't make me repeat myself.
Ugh—

PAPAS
CHURROS

VHS

Pedro Infante
is amazing here.

CALEXICO COMIC SHOP OPENS
Drug Smuggling Surges in
11
Imperial news

I just know I'd do better if I wasn't running errands all the time!
POWWW
Oh, c'mon. Your grade wasn't that bad.

My grade was sixty-five percent this time.
Yeah. It wasn't that bad.

Teresa is used to scoring ninety or higher. But it's gonna be fine.
It's just one monthly grade.

No! It's not just one monthly grade. What if that's the kind of student I am now?
POWWW

You're being very harsh on yourself. Caro is right.

My parents are going to kill me.
You can always not tell them—

Tell them how hard you're trying. It's not like they can't see it.

They don't care about that. They care about grades.

You could do what Chely did last year.
Remember, Nadia?

Nope!
PAHH!!!

Fine—last year
Chely also wanted to
raise her grade.

So she raised
money for a charity
in order to get
extra credit.

Did it
work?

I mean, the teacher
saw her efforts and it was
for one of the charities the
school supports, so—
yeah, it worked.

Yeah, I
guess I can give
that a try.

Here comes the birthday boy!

We're having a carne asada tonight with your uncles and aunts.
And tomorrow you get to celebrate in Imperial.

Happy birthday, Fer.

Happy birthday, twin.

Hey, you.
Hi!
PAPAS CHEMA

What's this?
Your birthday present, you dweeb. It's today, right?
PAPAS CHEMA
LIMON CON CHILE
Cumplea-
ÑeRo

Oh, thanks. Yeah, it is.

I remembered because it's the same day as the day of the Boy Heroes.

Not because I'm your friend, right?

Pff—one's more important, I guess.

HAPPY BIRTHDAY TO YOUUUU

The Holy Spirit brings you blessings

AND MANY MORE ON CHANNEL FOUR

Okay, everyone. Now in Spanish!

Thanks, everyone.

ESTAS SON LAS
MAÑANITAS- QUE
CANTABA EL REY
DAV -HOY POR
CUMPLEA-
From everyone in 7B!!
And that blessing is a
HAPPY BIRTHDAY
You're our favorite sibling!
BFFs
NADIA
YAY 7A

TE LAS CANTAMOS
AQUI! DESPIERTA
TED ESPIERT
AM

She's
THE WORST
teacher.

She's
AN AMAZING
teacher.

13

This is from us, and we hope you like it.
Just a little something for the Lu-lus.

Thanks, Uncle. Ehm...we don't use that nickname anymore.

Oh, I see. Sure. Do you have a cool new nickname?
Ja-ja, no. Just Teresa is fine.

Noted and done.

I liked our nickname.
Can I open my presents now?

We're going to do that after the cake.
Queremos Pastel Pastel Pastel-

Here.
I got you both the same thing, but in a different color.

Thank you, Aunt Laura.
Yeah! Thanks!

¡QUE LINDA ESTA LA MAÑANA EN QUE
¡LEVANTATE DE MAÑANA, MIRA QUE YA AMANECIÓ!

Chel's Tea Shop
WELCOME TO
EL CENTRO

IMPERIAL CINEMA
SHOWING
LOUIS XIV
THE LINE
I'm so excited!

The movie doesn't start for another hour.
I'm staying excited.
PIET
So how are you liking middle school, Fer?
It's okay. I have a lot of friends there.

Oh! They have a crane game now!
DTLA
CRANE
1-2
3-4
MAGIC IS HERE

It's her birthday! Help her!
MENU
GIANT PUZZLE

Did you already do the chemistry homework, Tony?
Yeah. It's very easy.
SOON
SAN DIEGO COMIC

Speak for yourself! The terms are so confusing.
No, it's super easy—
84
D.T.
08

Fer, you get chemistry, right?
COMING SOON
MAGIC IS HERE

MAGIC IS HERE
I kinda hate it.
NOW PLAYING

Oh—Teresa, do you also hate it?
25

I have my own opinions, Tony.
Yeah, get your own, Tony.
PICK UP PRIZE
PIET

What I mean is that Chemistry is fun—
That's why we don't like it: the fun.
EXIT

Maybe I just need help understanding it more.
I could help you with that.

I know a lot about chemistry. I even went to a summer camp a few weeks ago.
Really?

EXIT

Oh, there's my mom. See you later y'all. Teresa, happy birthday. Nice to meet you, Fernando.

Maggie, are you going to join us for the buffet?
Definitely! My dad will pick me up there at five.

I hope you kids had fun. Now let's go get something to eat.

The movie was great!
CASA BUFFET
Jacumba Casino

And at the end, I wasn't expecting to see multiple portals.
Right?
Me neither.
Menu
Kids' Buffet
CASA BUFFET

Do you go into Mexicali often?
Not too often. We go to San Felipe or Rosarito for spring break—

but my cousins love going into Mexicali for the weekend.

Are they all over eighteen?
YES!

Oh, so they go to bars and stuff—

Are there no bars in Calexico?

That's not why.

I still don't get it.

If I lived on this side, I'd be so happy not having to cross the border every day. Not having to answer weird questions to the cops.
Border agents aren't cops.
SAN DIEGO COMIC

They act like cops.

But their jobs are so different.
Yeah, they can't bust you for jaywalking.

Well, they're scary, and if I lived here, I wouldn't have to see them.

Oh, we see them all the time. It's weird to see them watching people who talk to their family through the fence.
SAN DIEGO

Or if you stayed in Mexicali, you wouldn't cross every day.

I'm getting more food. Do you want more nuggets, Caro?
I'll get some in a bit.
I'm just saying—
SKAREN
if crossing is such an issue, why not just—
not do it?
We have everything awesome in Mexicali.
I dunno... The movie we just saw won't come to Mexico for a while, if ever.
And the malls? No contest. Over here we have San Diego and Viejas outlet.
Mexico has way better movies. Ever heard of Cine de Oro?
I mean, we do have our downsides, like, Mexicali is bigger and has more—
It has a LOT more stuff. Mundo Divertido? A zoo? Fiestas del Sol? What do you have over here? Nothing!

My family is moving here by Christmas.

How was the movie?

Fer ruins everything and I wish he had stayed here.

I just told the truth and you hate facts!

That's not even true!
Whoa whoa what happened with those two?
Und
Const

Was the movie not good?

Fernando made a scene at the buffet and now he's no longer friends with Tony.
But why is Teresa upset?

Just give them space, will you?

Wanna tell me why your brother is upset with you?

Upset with me? Are you SERIOUS? He's the one who–

Whoa whoa there, missy. I just asked you a question.
But Fer was yelling at my friends–

Calm down. Look, why don't we go to a quermés tonight and forget all about it.
No!

Teresa, it's going to make you feel better.

I don't want to go.

Where are we going?
NO ONE IS TALKING TO YOU!

We're thinking of going to a quermés. Do you want to go?

I really don't wanna go anywhere right now.

We should go.
Let's go, then.

BUÑUELOS
BROCHETAS
TORTAS

COCTELES
$5

AZUCAR
You missed out last night, Teresa.
FIESTA

Tonight's the big night. We're going to the civic center around eight, so all your homework should be done by then.
Can I skip out on tonight's celebration?

It's Independence Day, dear. You have to come celebrate.
ARINA

But I have school tomorrow. The Grito is not until midnight. I can't stay up that late.
I don't have school tomorrow.

I know you don't. But I do.

It's no big deal. We'll come home immediately after the Grito.
But I have to be up so early, Dad.

So right after the Grito, we come home and you get a good night's sleep for tomorrow.
Mom? Can I skip out this time?

RING-RING-RING
The Grito is so awesome and then the fireworks castle?
FIESTAS 94

Hello? Oh, hello, Alex.
Yes, he's right here.
FIESTAS

Fernando, it's for you.

Hello? Oh, hey! No, I haven't heard it. Yeah, let's hang out and listen to it.

JUEGOS
FRESCAS
Cerveza 686
SOPES
TAMALES
EL TATEMADO
CHEVE

CACHANILLA

¡VIVA MÉXICO!
¡¡VIVA LA INDEPENDENCIA!!
¡¡¡VIVAN LOS HEROES!!!
1810

SAN FELIPE
JMP

1810
VIVA

Mom, I'm very tired.
ONTIER

Bye, Mom.

Here are the chocolates you can sell for extra credit.

Can I take two boxes?

Do you wanna go sell chocolates door to door with me?
Sure!

Hey, Alex.
Are we still hanging out tomorrow?
Yeah, you know I'm very cool.
Okay. See you tomorrow.

His murals are amazing. They speak to what's going on, and his style is so rad.
Have you seen the one by Casa de la Cultura? It's huge.
TMN
ALTO
Yaqui

The one that spells "Mexicali" and inside the letters you see a lot of landmarks?
YEAH! I mean, it's on the nose—

Like, the "MEXI" part has nature—

and the "CALI" has, like, fast food landmarks and gross American things— but I dig it.

Why are murals such a big deal?

Because art should be for people. We have to see it. It has to be big.

I guess... graffiti is like newer murals.

Exactly! So they gotta have a message. A bold message.
Hey! Let's make a mural combining our photos.
What would you title it?
TORRES

Oh, there's people–

That's a crummy title–
No, I mean–

There's people coming this way.

Oh no! That's my sister.
You have a younger sister?

Pff—no. She's my twin sister.
Is she cool?

Well—

Hi, Teresa.
We're fine. This is Alex.
That's Caro. We're fine.

Hey. What are you two up to?

You're his twin.
Is that weird sometimes?

I'm gonna head on home. I'll see you there, Fer.

I see she's not as cool as you.

Oh, well. I'm also gonna head home. Get mural ideas for the people.
Later.

Yeah... Later.

What?

What kind of question is that to ask someone?
What?
That "Is it weird" thing?

That's not what you ask someone you've just met!

Oh! He was just being funny.

Maybe you should try it sometime.

That wasn't funny. He was very rude!
You're rude!

You're acting very weird and I don't like it.

Well, maybe we're both weird.

Look, I'm tired of going door to door selling these chocolates. I'm going home.
Saint Chocolates

Oh! Do you have some with almonds?

They're a dollar each.

$1.00
Saint Chocolate
ALMOND

$1.00

206
That's that smell, remember?

I'm- Sorry

Choco lates

Thanks for your company.
No problem. I'll see you tomorrow.

How did it go, Teresa?
It went well. We bumped into Fer and Alex.

We weren't doing anything!

I'm going to go to Mass later this evening. Do any of you want to join me?
I'm sorry, Mom. I really want to, but I have a lot of homework to do.
Yeah. We have a lot of homework to do.
If you had done your homework earlier, it wouldn't be an issue.
I have religion class tomorrow. That counts.
No it doesn't.
Well, your dad is not going, so I guess you kids can stay here.

So all of your teachers are nuns?
Catecismo

Huh. We have a nun to teach us religion class. But it's mostly about one religion.
Most of them.

Do you have that class every day?
Nah.
That's too bad.

You'd like that every day?

Yeah. It's important to me. That's why I'm hoping to get into a Catholic high school...
...and why I'd like to go to a Catholic college.

You don't think the whole thing is silly?

No. It fulfills me.

I dunno. I'm looking forward to high school, where we don't have a religion class.
Well, I think it's important to educate my soul.

Meh.

Mom!
Mom!
I got invited to a slumber party this weekend!
I can go, right?
Can I go? Can I go?

Hello. Nice to see you. How was school?
Yeah, hi. But I can go, right?

It's gonna be super fun!
Mom, I haven't had a sleepover since I was six.
Well...

And this is at Maggie's house, so it's gonna be super cool—
Doesn't Maggie live in Calexico?

Well, yeah—

Your father and I will have to discuss it.
ATLAS

What if I get super awesome grades and I do more chores?

It's not about that, honey. It's about you sleeping on the other side.

Maggie's parents are so responsible and we're not going anywhere.

Your dad and I will discuss it.
What's there to discuss?
ATLAS

I wanna go to a slumber party.
Hey, that's not fair. If she goes, I can go to a slumber party, too.
You're not invited to this slumber party.
I have friends, too, you know.
You have, like, one weirdo friend.
Okay, you two, that's enough. Teresa, I will discuss it with your dad when he gets home.
And, Fernando? If Teresa gets to go, you can arrange a sleepover if you'd like. But you have to organize it.

I can't believe you'd let Alex come to this house.

That's enough, Teresa.

He's your brother's friend.

Now both of you go wash your hands. We're gonna eat soon.
ATLAS

Alex is not a weirdo.

He's trouble waiting to happen.
You'll see.
Pfft–
CALEXICO
SAM ELLIS

Then, on a trip to a bookstore, I saw them collected in book form, and I've been buying them since.

Ja-ja.
Ja-ja.
These guys dance funny.

Yeah. I love how they combine folk rhythms, but it sounds like rock music. It doesn't feel old. It's unique.
VHS

Oh, this next song is terrible-let's check the MTV channel.

Nah—they play a lot of American music. Let's see what movie is playing on channel five.

They don't just play American stuff.

I know. Sometimes they play Brit-pop, and that's okay.
But I'd rather just not. It's still an American company.
5
ESTAS VIENDO

Okay. I wanted to surprise you three with something my dad just got.

Oooh. Suspense.

TA-DA!!!
PLAYBOX
PLAYBOX 2K

NO WAY!

THAT'S AWESOME!

HOW?! HOW DID YOU GET ONE?

Wow, you really go far to avoid the other side, huh?

Do you dislike them that much?

I HATE THEM.

Right now, the only games are single player, but I thought we could take turns.
Well, you have to go first. It's your game.

Actually, I was hoping one of you would go first. I learn better by watching.
I totally wanna go first.

Why don't we have a disparejo to figure out who goes first?
Good idea.

¡DIS-PA-RE-

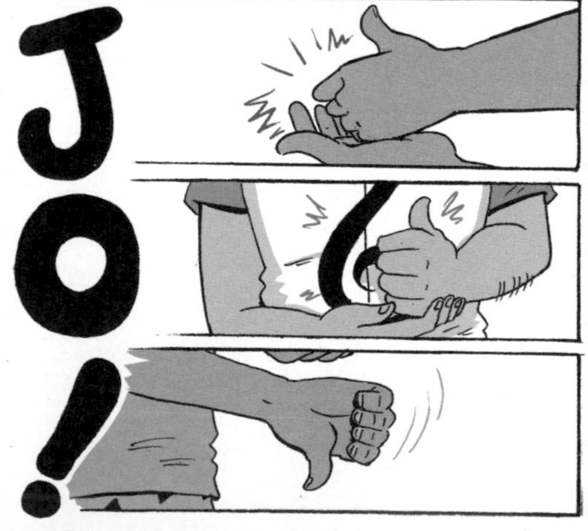
JO!

You go first, Teresa.

They like to come here and party, but they won't let us go twenty-five miles north—

without interrogating us about every little detail because they can.

They claim to like our culture, but they only want to collect it. They like our look, but they hate us.
They won't be happy until we fully assimilate to their lifestyle.

And even then, they'll be angry that we're here.

They'll say that they're the ones bringing the money—

so they should get to have a say—

in how things are done.

Minas de
SINALOA

YEAH! YEAH!
GO GO GO GO

YES!!! THAT'S AWESOME WHOA!!

WOO!
GET IT GET

C'MON C'MON

OH NO—OH NO—OH NO—

LEVEL UP

Minas de
SINALOA
They say we live in a culture clash here, but it's an invasion—
and I know they don't want us. Not there, not here, not ever.

Yes, I hate them. Just like they've always hated us.

If I had a say, that fence would be solid and sky-high.
Maybe then, everyone here would realize that we don't need them.

They just want us to want them.
With their generic food—

Whoa. Food sounds good right now.
Yeah! Let's grab something.

I'm never getting bored of this game!

It's as fun as trying on makeup.

You try on makeup?

You don't try on makeup?

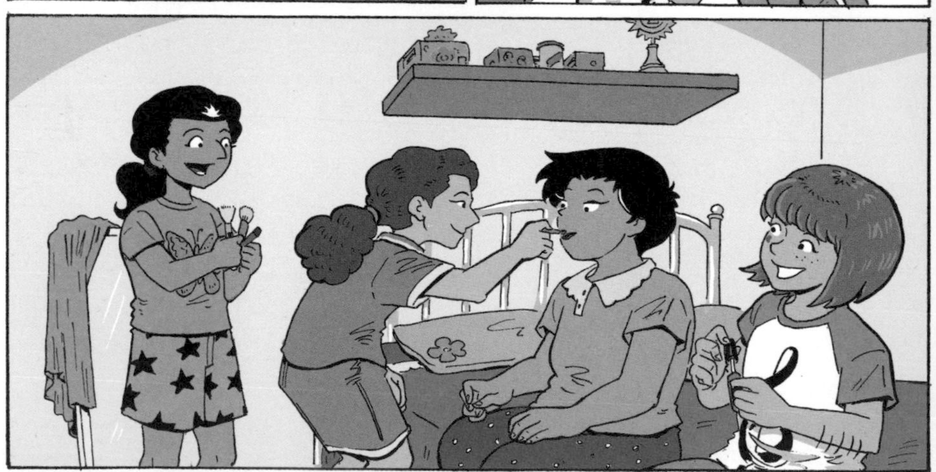

Have you always felt that way?
I didn't used to think much about them.

Then I had to go and live there for a bit and it was the worst.

Like, did they call you names and stuff? Because that would explain the occasional fistfight.
Names I could deal with. It's the other stuff, like saying they'll call the Migra. Or looking at us like criminals.
PAPAS CHEMA

And then there's all the pochos over there who want to forget where they came from. They're just as bad.
And their schools are weird. When I came back, I had to repeat a year.

I should be a grade higher.
Is that how you get invited to quinceañeras?
That, and my supplier is in high school.
Supplier?

She's obviously the best. She gets a magic carpet at the end and has a tiger. Easy choice.
Sorry, I'd go for the library.
Does the lioness count? She is royalty.
I mean, she should.
Is she your favorite?
No, but I like the option.
I like sleeping, so you know my answer.

Where do you think I get my stash? I keep some, but it's for selling.
PAPAS CHEMS

But that's illegal, isn't it?
It's a gray area.

Plus, it's nice to have your own money.

I guess it's good, since your parents are out of town so often.
Yup.
C'mon. Let's watch a Capulina movie.

What's a pocho?
BWA-JA-JA-JA

I haven't slept in a sleeping bag in ages.
My dad takes me camping often, so I'm used to it.

I sleep on a futon on the floor every day, so this is normal for me.

What? Why?
Oh, because my room is not finished, so I sleep in the TV room.

Every night?

So do you want to make money?
It's really easy. Think about it.
What? No. I mean, yes, but not right—

You can have your own money for whatever you want.

I wouldn't even know what to do.
Let me handle that. For now, all you gotta do is hold it for me.

And at school, come with me when I'm selling. It's always good to have an extra person.
Also, if you wanna try and meet some of the kids on your block, we can split things in half.
We can be the cool duo.

One more before we go?

Hee-hee-hee.
And then she says: "You WAFFLE like a duck!"
Ha ha ha!
That's so silly!

This was great. When can we do it again?

You sleep like a rock.
Did you rest well?
I was so tired.
Yeah.

So, about what I brought up last night—
Well, I do like us being a duo. That sounds cool.

Yeah! Look, take these and give it a shot.

Just don't lose them, because I already owe a bit to my dealer.

For what?
Where were you last night? This stuff isn't free.
But seriously, you and I?

We're a team now.

Hi, Mom!
FRONTIER
Clip!
Let's spend the morning here in Calexico.

30%
DESCUENTO
Sam Ellis Store
20%

Let's get a donut.
CASA DE CAMBIO
PIXE
OPEN
Las Mejores
•Coffee
•Sandwiches
•Bagels
•Pan Dulce
tel. 760-38

I'll see you tomorrow, carnal.
Totally. See ya then.

Hi, Fer. Let's go get some breakfast.
Yeah!

Merendero
MANUET

Hi!
Hey!

You won't believe what happened last night.
What?

We got to play PlayBox 2K!

Whoa— that's SO—

I mean, that's cool.

What are we watching?
An action movie. It's hard to take seriously when it's dubbed, though.

No, it makes it more fun. Plus, I understand the jokes a lot better.

I see, but it takes me out of it.
Like, I know that's not their real voice.

It's the same voice for every main character and the voice for every funny character.

It's less real.

It's an action movie. It's already not real.

Hey!
I was watching that!

I got here first.
And you don't even ask?

What do you even want to watch?

Maybe there's something better on Imperial channels.
Just because it's on an American channel doesn't mean it's better.

I have the remote so I choose.

Wow. October hasn't even started and they're already showing these?

I know, right? It's like they can't stop saying, "Buy this, buy that." Ugh—
Hee-hee-hee.

I like Day of the Dead better anyways.

Oh, no way. Halloween is way more fun. And you get candy.

You get candy on Day of the Dead, too.
C'mon! No contest.
Pan de muerto is covered in sugar, but it's no trick-or-treating.

Day of the Dead actually MEANS something. Halloween is just shallow.

No, it has—
some history.
Like what? Buy some cheap overpriced costume and get generic candy bars?

Well, which one is it?
Cheap or overpriced?

You know what I mean. And it's not even celebrating anything.

It's for friends to get together and get candy.

We have authentic music! Ceremonies! Family traditions!
All that excuse of a holiday has is "Ooohh, we're scary—oooh."
It's dumb!

Oh, you're an expert on music now?

I know it's better than that gringo pop.
And what are we even watching on this channel?
A pointless cartoon with no message?

What Mexican cartoon has a message?
In fact, what Mexican cartoons are there? NONE.

Plenty! But you don't care because you're turning into a total pocha.

POCHA?
You watch dubs because your English is terrible and you don't want to learn anything!
That's why you have no friends and why nobody LIKES YOU!

KDM

Oh, This isn't over, Luis Fernando Sosa. I'm gonn-

SLAM!

Oh-
nder
ruction

YOU AS-

I don't care what he said. We don't use those words here.
I'm very disappointed in you.

But he was be–

–ing so mean.

rrRIIIPpp

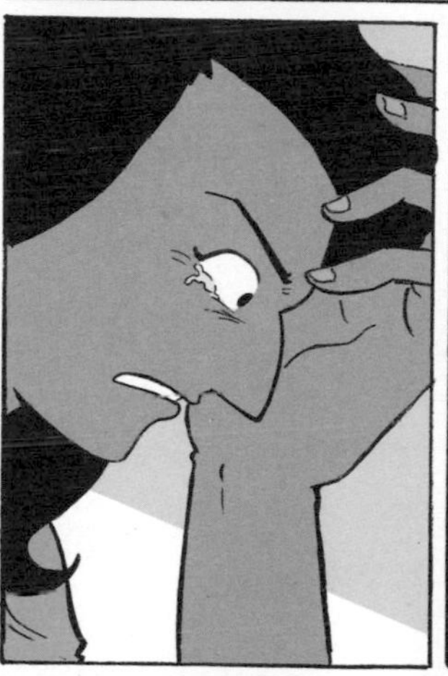

SNIFF
SNIFF
SNIFF

SNIFF-SNIFF-SNIFF-SNIFF-SNIFF-SNIFF-SNI---
KDM
KDM
ZIP!

KNOCK
KNOCK

Luis Fernando?

Can I come in and talk to you?

KDM

KDM

He's still upset. But he owes you an apology.

Just let him blow off some steam for now.
Mom, he—

I know, I know. He said awful things.

But he's just going through a tough time right now.

HE is going through a tough time?

Mom! I'm having a tough time, too!

Look, Teresa, if you're not going to be understanding—
MOM!

Okay, well, clearly you need more time to think about what you said.

And clean your space.

PASAPORTE
MEXICO
Bye, Mom.
AYUDA
FRONTIER

TRANSITO LOCAL
MEDICAL LANE
LINEA INTERNACIONAL
CALEXICO/USA
AUTOBUSES
MOTOR HOMES
RVs
PIGA

CLIP!
CLIP!

Taking the kids to school?
Hmmm...
Okay...
Sir, you have been selected for secondary inspection.
Drive that way.

Follow the officer.

Stop there.

Step over to the waiting area.

Where did
I put my-
Oh, right.
KDM

Bye, Mom!

KDM

WAIT HERE
ESPERE AQUI
Move it along. Hurry up.

Do you think we'll be late? 'Cause I have a test.

What was the issue, officer?
There is no issue. You may move along.

FISICA

HISTORIA

No way...

Luisa Teresa, you jerk...

TURY
1903
PIRA
TITO'S
CAR REPAIR
US
POST

ON
Fernando Sosa?
HISTORIA
Sorry. What was the question?
LUNes:

2.3
Trajan's Column
Science
Algebra
2y+2=
30+2=
Y=
Are you listening?
Sorry. What was the question?

DWLAAP!

FRONTIER

Oh, you too?

Mom, I REALLY don't feel well.

Let me feel your forehead.
My stomach hurts a lot and I can't walk good.

Walk well.

I can't!

No, it's "I can't walk—"
Never mind.

I can't do this right now.

I have to go to work and you have to go to school.
Mom, I'm going to throw up.

Ugh—stay here.

Well, you missed your car pool. How are you feeling?

My head is throbbing and I feel dizzy.

Okay. Rest and I'll check up on you later.

Hello?
Yeah?
I'm not going to make it.
No, everything is fine.
Both of my kids are sick today.
Yeah.
Mm-hmm.
I have the files here.
I can work here and just come over when I'm finished.
Thank you for understanding.
Kids! I'm going to be in the kitchen. I'll check on you in a few minutes.
Okay, then.

Pocket-sized dictionary.
English
E
S

It's past two o'clock. Are you feeling any better?
A little better. But I think I don't want to go to school tomorrow, either.

Well, if you're still sick, we'll go to the doctor. But if you're not sick, you have to go.

But what if I'm not sick, but still...don't want to go?

Oh, Teresa, you really

How's your head?

It still hurts.
I thought it was your stomach.

It's both, Mom!

Of course.
I have to go and drop off these files. Keep resting.

I'll be back in less than an hour, Teresa. Don't get in trouble while I'm gone.
Okay.

Hi, Tia Sosa! Is Fer home?

Oh, hi, Alex. He is, but he's not supposed to receive visitors right now.
He'll be in school tomorrow. Have a good afternoon.
Aww, not even me?
Oh. Okay. You too, Tia.

Thank you!

KNOCK
KNOCK

I just saw you.

TAP TAP TAP

What's up?
Hey. How are you?

You're avoiding me.
No, I'm n—

It wasn't a question.

Who's in here?

Oh, hey.
This is none of your business, so leave.

I live here, and what are YOU doing here?

So you're avoiding me.
What's up?

I, ehm–

What?

I lost 'em.

You what?
I lost them.

What do you mean—

you lost them?

I guess I might have dropped them somewhere. But I lost them.

Is that all? That's why you're avoiding me?
Yeah.

Aw, don't worry about it. Just pay me for them.

What?
I made it clear, Fernando. Pay me back or pay me back.
I don't have any—
That's not my problem. Rob someone, shoplift somewhere, or steal it from your parents. I don't care. But you're paying me back.
But I don't—
AHH!!
HOLY—
I don't think you're understanding what I'm telling you. And I don't like repeating myself.
PAY ME NOW.
PERIOD.

GET OFF OF HIM!
AHHHGGGggg
ARE YOU GOING TO PAY ME, FER?
BACK OFF, MORRA!
HUFF
HUFF
HUFF
gr-grgrgr

HERE!

Aw, look at this.

Just take it and go away.

hmm..hmmm...
mmm...

This should do it.

What is this?
I'm taking what he lost.

I'm not a thief.

And you?

Don't ever come near me, you wimp.

Are you okay?

Yeah, I'm good.

STOP LYING!

You're NOT okay. It's obvious that you're not okay!

And you're hiding in your room because you're too afraid to face what YOU did!

And YOU did a thing that could have gotten you in JAIL! And there were other KIDS in the car!

Balboa Park

Wait, what car?
Do you have ANY idea HOW DUMB IT IS TO HAVE THAT STUFF IN YOUR BACKPACK?
I KNEW YOU TOOK IT!

DUH! YOU'RE MAKING DUMB CHOICES!
Oh, I've been making dumb choices?
You're the one who's only thinking of abandoning everything because-
"I wanna study in gringolandia."
It's the US, Fernando. There're opportunities.
There will be opportunities here!
HERE?
I don't even have my own room!

Soon you'll have—
It's been two years, Fernando.

I've been sleeping without a door for two years. I want my OWN space.

ANYWHERE.
You have a room with a desk and YOU DON'T EVEN USE IT!

But do you have to be so desperate to leave?

It's like, ever since you got into that school, you don't wanna do any of the stuff we used to have fun doing.

I have fun doing stuff! It's just that... sometimes that means without...
...you.

SEE? You have friends!

Dalboa
You...also have friends.
I HAD a friend who's gone now!

That jerk who took my charity money wasn't a FRIEND, Fernando.

He was MY friend.

Well, I'm your friend.

You're my sister.

Well, it's not like you've been a...nice brother lately.

I could really use support. This is all very hard.

What...do you want?

Privacy. But also to know you're on my side sometimes.

Dad's advice is terrible and Mom can be difficult to talk to.

I want... someone here to just listen.

Dad does give bad advice sometimes.

SO bad. And Mom? Can she listen for a minute?

Why? She's already made up her mind.

I KNOW!!

I'm sorry
I called you
a pocha.
It hurt a lot.
I want space
for me, but—
that's the
furthest
I've ever felt
from you.
I want
us to stay
close.

I can be close.

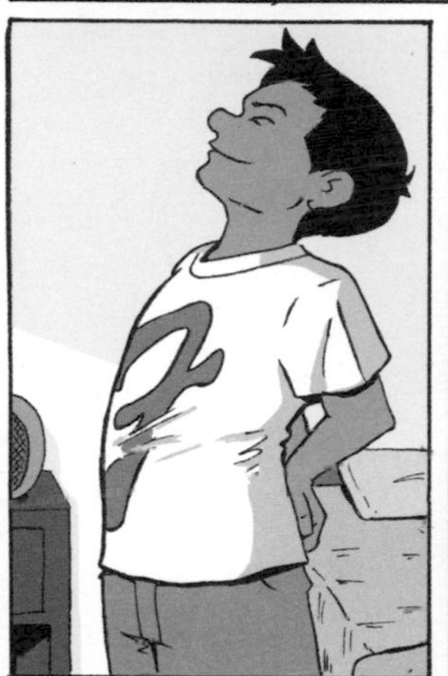

I can give you space.
Just promise you won't forget where you come from.

Promise me you'll help me go through this—
new school stuff.

Deal!
Deal!

Oh, I see both of you are feeling better.
TEN

Move it. You're not wasting the rest of the day.

You might as well help me around the house.

Michoacana
PASAPORTE
FRONTIER

Hey, Fer.

What are you eating today?

CHECK OUT THE NEW PIZZA FLAVOR!

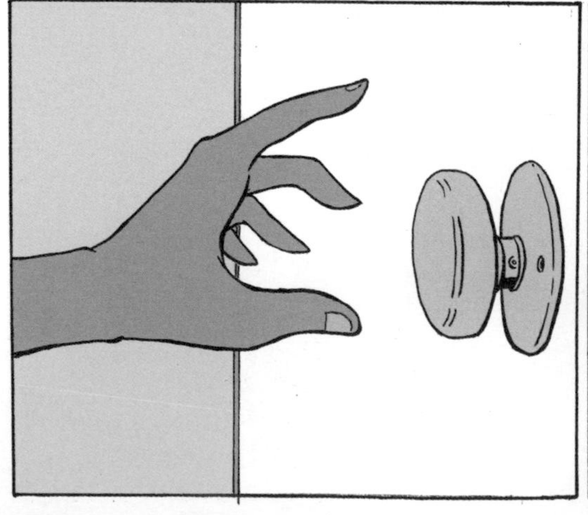

Hey, you.

Hi there.

Today's the day.

It is a big day.

Wanna come check it out?

Mmm—I'll join you later. I really wanna get this.

MY ROO
MY RULE
7A

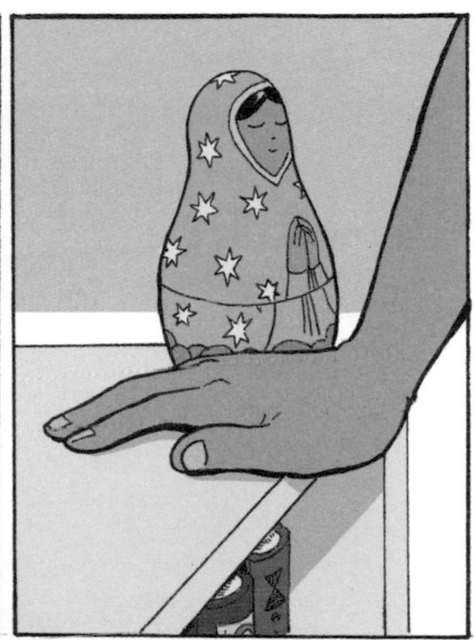

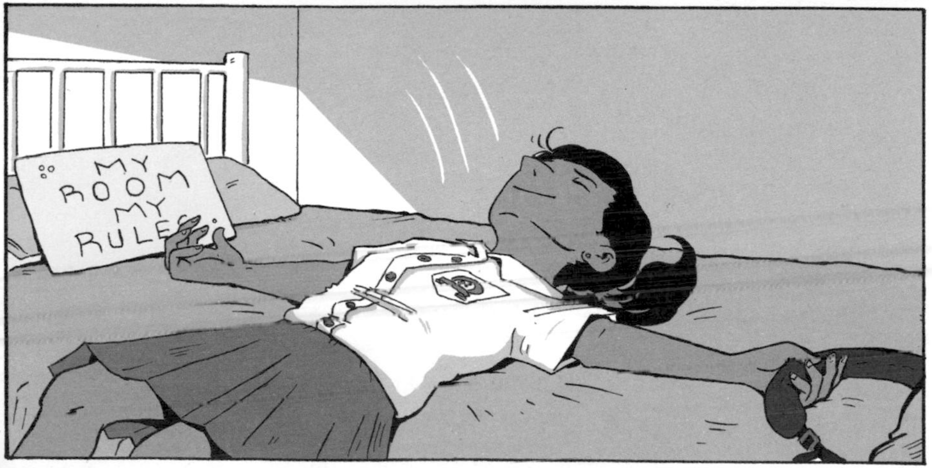
MY ROOM MY RULES

Hey, Fer!

Come in here for a second.

What?
MY ROOM MY RULE

I'd like your expertise.

I have all this wall space and a window now. Should I hang posters? Or photos?
MY ROOM MY RULES

Hmmm-

Kids! Get ready to eat.

# A Very Personal Note

*Twin Cities* came from a concept so simple that it remains the tagline: Mexicali twins continue their middle school education on opposite sides of the border.

I chose middle schools in Mexicali and Calexico as a setting because I had a similar experience. When I finished sixth grade, my parents presented me with the option of studying in the United States. They told me it would make it easier if I ever wanted to attend high school or college on the American side. If I didn't like it, I could come back to finish middle school. I decided to stay on the Mexican side because my friends were there. But I still wonder what would have happened had I made a different choice.

My siblings had different experiences. My brother went to middle school in Calexico but finished high school in Mexico. My sister spent most of her academic life in Calexico and went to an American college. As siblings do, we often compared notes on the pros and cons of each school. We also compared the Mexican school system with the American one. WIthout knowing it, we were generalizing two countries to make sense of our day-to-day lives. We shared stories about teachers, parts of the school that we were familiar with, and the advantages of getting up earlier or getting home sooner. A lot of families go through similar situations. As I was writing this book, I wanted to examine some of those moments and figure out what was at the core of them. Little to no surprise, it is a combination of things.

Siblinghood is complex. For many, siblings are the people who watch us grow as they grow alongside us. They live under the same roof, so territoriality can be an unspoken force for peace or downright war. From food to toys to who gets to choose the channel or who gets to ride in the front seat, bargains are made or conflict ensues. Our siblings can be the people in whom we most confide but also the ones who know how we are the most vulnerable. They have a unique position in our lives; we do not choose them, but we can choose to keep them. They are not our ancestry nor our individuality, but they can reflect where we come from—sometimes more bluntly than we'd like. And yet, they can be our rocks. Our champions. They can remind us without effort of what we have gone through and how we could be better. Siblings, especially at a young age, are the people who first show us that we can be different and unique while still sharing traits and worldviews. Siblings grow together, which means they can branch out while remaining tethered.

Writing this book also put me in a position to explore things that I've been dealing with for a very long time. I was born in the Imperial Valley, but I grew up on the Mexican side. I watched American television but listened to Mexican music. I went to American concerts but ate Mexican food. My passport says one thing, but my heritage says another. Even when I was as young as the characters in *Twin Cities*, I had questions but lacked the vocabulary to articulate them. I wanted to explore something I still experience through these characters—not just Teresa and Fernando but their friends and parents as well.

The longer I live in the United States, the more distant I feel from my Mexicali upbringing. Not just because I get older. I love getting older and discovering new interests. But I can't help but notice some things dim in the distance or become unrecognizable. This is for things such as TV shows, music, or a type of humor. But it can also be for deeper matters such as friendships or customs. To consider that my hometown and my language may be among those things sometimes terrifies me, so I have to make efforts to continue cultivating them. I have to make efforts to continue to carry some of those elements I love. *Twin Cities* was one of those efforts. In a way, one of my intentions with *Twin Cities* was to remind myself why Mexicali is special but why I chose to leave. I wanted to express thanks for all the good times, the shortcomings, and the valuable lessons of growing up in a border city with strong people all around. I hope this book gets that point across.

When I was growing up, crossing the border was easy and quick. We even had jokes that one city was the extension of the other, no difference between the two. The other side of that coin was to joke about how we behaved differently as soon as we crossed that border line. Over the past few years, the physical barriers between Mexicali and Calexico have become more rigid. Working on this book was a constant reminder of the growing emphasis on the differences between the two nations instead of the similarities the people share. It's painful. Still, this project was my vessel to visit Mexicali and the Imperial Valley. Despite my unfavorable opinion about the desert's weather, I feel nothing short of pride and praise for Mexicali and Calexico. Mexicali held the world record for the largest taco in the early 2000s; it's the only border city where the Mexican side has a larger city than the American side; and its best feature is the people. I don't visit as frequently as I would like to. However, I stay in touch with relatives and friends who give me updates and recommendations on what to eat or where to go the next time I swing by. And as soon as I'm there, I smile. It's where I'm from, and it's where a lot of wonderful people live.

I should also note that for younger cities, Mexicali and Calexico are abundant with immigrant and native stories. I highlight Chinese food as the regional food, but the history of the Chinese community is a pillar to the region, yet it's not my story to tell. I recommend looking into it since it's also tied to the history of the United States. Likewise, local indigenous communities of the Baja peninsula have a rich culture tied to the land. They are their own storytellers and must have recognition for history through their lens. They have been here the longest and know the land better than most. I rarely touch on the subject but am trying to learn more from them.

# CHARACTERS

## Luisa Teresa Sosa

Born on September 13, she's a girl who has recently developed an interest in studying in the United States. She's not afraid to ask a question when she's feeling uncertain and enjoys talking to her friends during lunch. She loves video games and candy. She also has a tendency to not finish her food. Since Teresa grew up as a twin, she's accustomed to being treated as half of a unit. But she's learning to set boundaries that let people know she wants to be her own person. She's even leaving her old nickname, "Lu-lu Twin," behind in order to claim full autonomy of her identity. Her favorite color is blue, and she loves Mexicali's Chinese food.

TERESA

# Luis Fernando Sosa

**Born on September 13, he's a bit on the shy side and likes things the way they are. He doesn't enjoy mowing the lawn, which his father makes him do on a regular basis. He prefers to watch television and play video games. He also loves taking photographs and turning them into a collage. Unlike his twin sister, he loves being treated as half of a unit. He may think he's the better half, but he's happy being half of a Lu-lu Twin. His interest in school has less to do with his classes and more to do with seeing his friends. He loves corn chips, Mexicali's Chinese food, and any Mexican candy. Fernando is also left-handed.**

# SKETCHES

HALLWAY
to
Kitchen
opening
Power strip
FeR's
Room
Room
under Construction
HALLWAY
Phone
BACK door

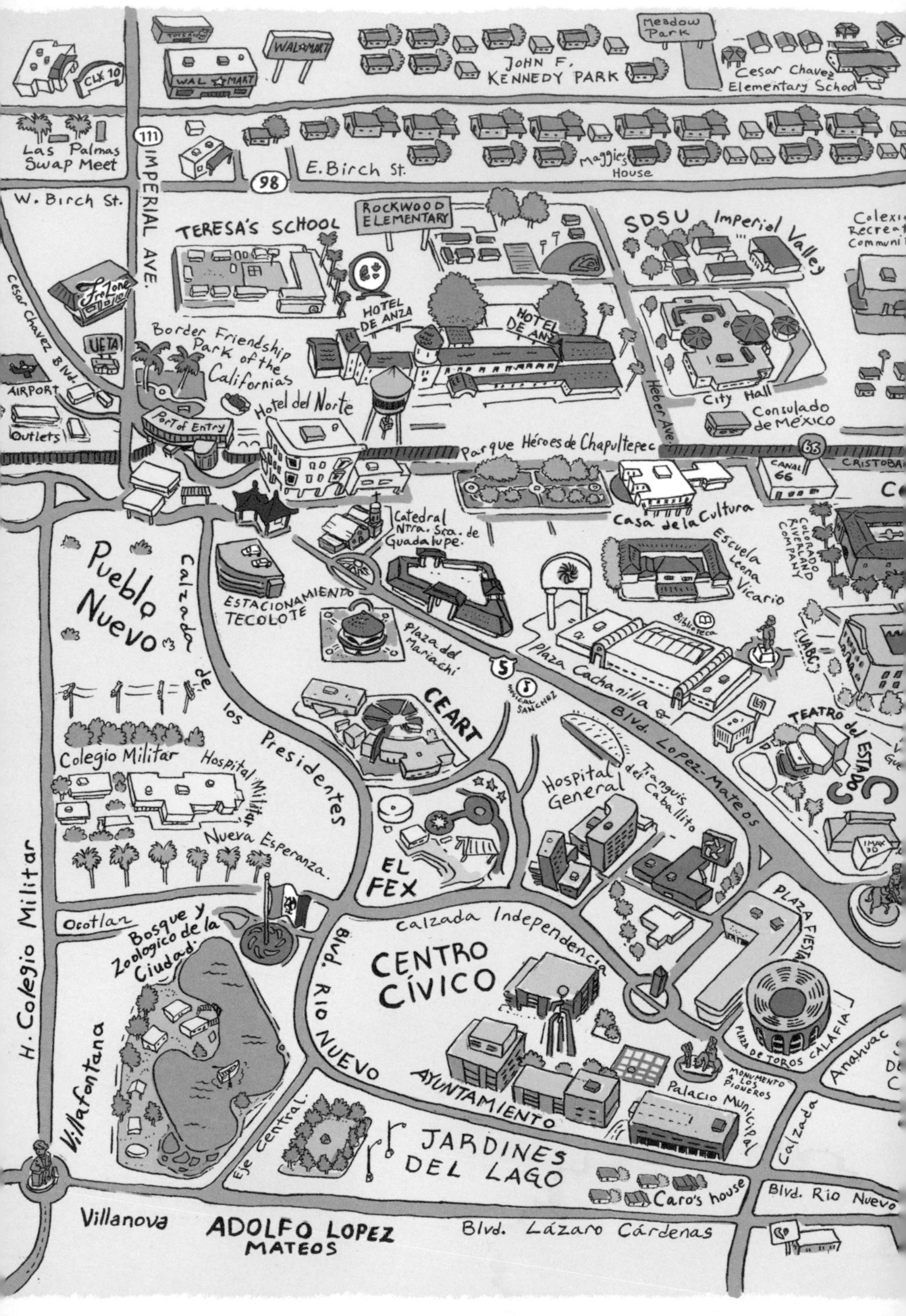

CLX 10
WAL★MART
WALMART
JOHN F. KENNEDY PARK
Meadow Park
Cesar Chavez Elementary School
Las Palmas Swap Meet
111
IMPERIAL AVE.
98
E. Birch St.
Maggie's House
W. Birch St.
ROCKWOOD ELEMENTARY
TERESA'S SCHOOL
SDSU Imperial Valley
Cesar Chavez Blvd.
HOTEL DE ANZA
HOTEL DE ANZA
Border Friendship Park of the Californias
AIRPORT
Outlets
Port of Entry
Hotel del Norte
Heber Ave.
City Hall
Consulado de México
Parque Héroes de Chapultepec
66
CANAL 66
CRISTOBA
Casa de la Cultura
Catedral Ntra. Sra. de Guadalupe
COLORADO RIVER LAND COMPANY
Escuela Leona Vicario
Pueblo Nuevo
Calzada de los Presidentes
ESTACIONAMIENTO TECOLOTE
Plaza del Mariachi
Biblioteca
UABC
Plaza Cachanilla
5
MUSICAL SANCHEZ
CEART
Blvd. Lopez-Mateos
TEATRO del ESTADO
Colegio Militar
Hospital Militar
Hospital General
Tianguis del Caballito
Nueva Esperanza.
EL FEX
PLAZA FIESTA
H. Colegio Militar
Ocotlan
Bosque y Zoologico de la Ciudad
Calzada Independencia
CENTRO CÍVICO
Blvd. Rio Nuevo
PLAZA DE TOROS CALAFIA
Anahuac
Villafontana
AYUNTAMIENTO
MONUMENTO A LOS PIONEROS
Palacio Municipal
Calzada
Eje Central
JARDINES DEL LAGO
Caro's house
Blvd. Rio Nuevo
Villanova
ADOLFO LOPEZ MATEOS
Blvd. Lázaro Cárdenas

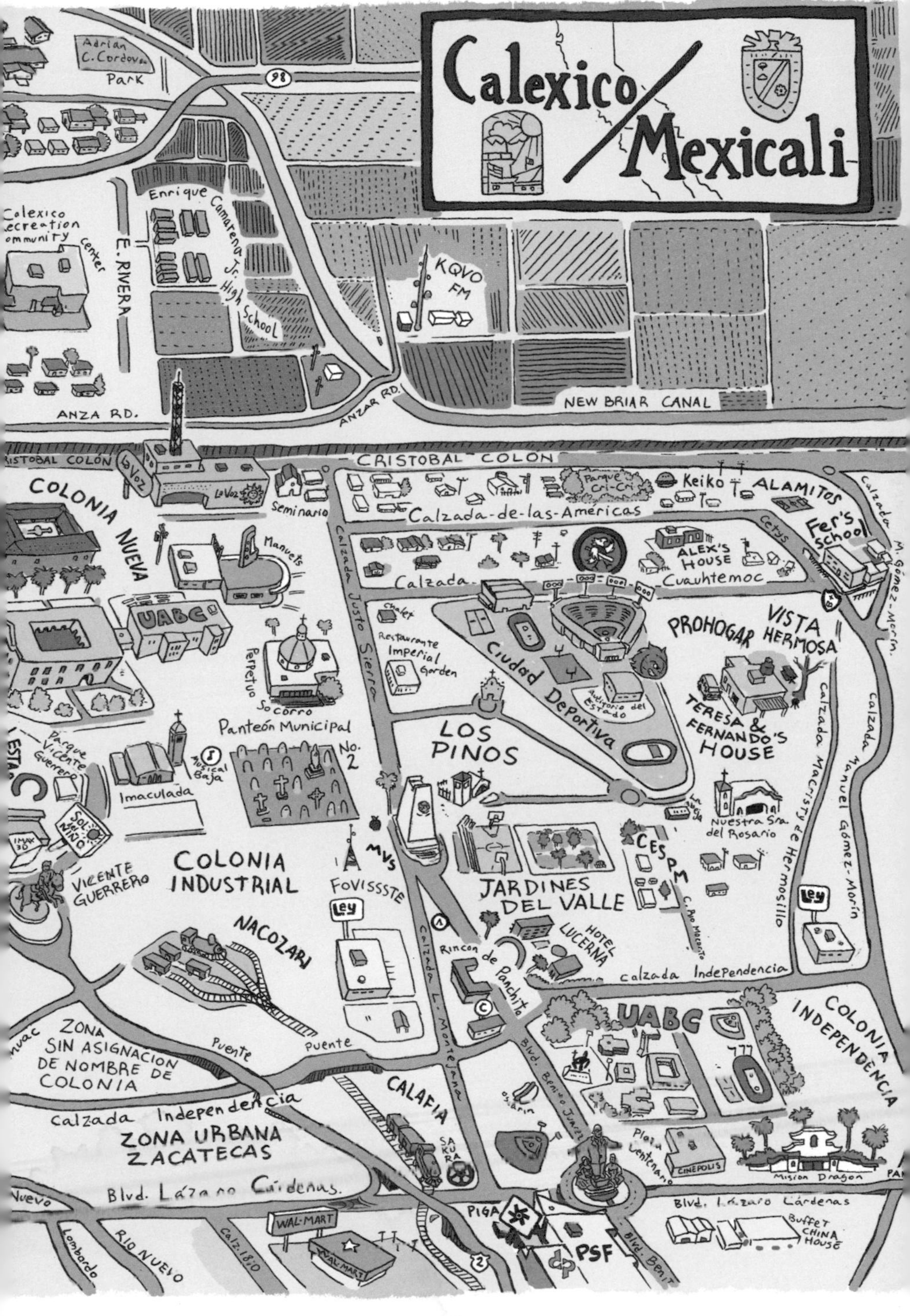

Calexico
Mexicali
Adrian C. Cordova Park
98
Calexico Recreation Community Center
E. RIVERA
Enrique Camarena Jr. High School
KQVO FM
ANZA RD.
ANZAR RD.
NEW BRIAR CANAL
CRISTOBAL COLÓN
La Voz
COLONIA NUEVA
Seminario
Manuels
UABC
Perpetuo Socorro
Panteón Municipal No. 2
Parque Vicente Guerrero
Musical Baja
Imaculada
SOL DEL NIÑO
IMAX 3D
VICENTE GUERRERO
COLONIA INDUSTRIAL
NACOZARI
ZONA SIN ASIGNACION DE NOMBRE DE COLONIA
Puente
Calzada Independencia
ZONA URBANA ZACATECAS
Blvd. Lázaro Cárdenas
Nuevo
Lombardo
RIO NUEVO
Calz. 18 O
WAL-MART
Calzada Justo Sierra
Parque Cri-Cri
Keiko
ALAMITOS
Calzada-de-las-Americas
Cetys
Fer's School
ALEX'S HOUSE
Calzada Cuauhtemoc
Chalet
Restaurante Imperial Garden
Ciudad Deportiva
Auditorio del Estado
PROHOGAR
VISTA HERMOSA
TERESA & FERNANDO'S HOUSE
LOS PINOS
Nuestra Sra. del Rosario
CESPM
MVS
FOVISSSTE
Ley
JARDINES DEL VALLE
HOTEL LUCERNA
C. Rio Mocorito
Rincon de Panchito
Calzada L. Montejano
calzada Independencia
Calzada Macristy de Hermosillo
Calzada Manuel Gómez-Morín
Calzada M. Gómez-Morín
COLONIA INDEPENDENCIA
UABC
Blvd. Benito Juarez
CALAFIA
SAKURA
Plaza Centenario
CINEPOLIS
Mision Dragon
PIGA
PSF
Blvd. Benit
Blvd. Lázaro Cárdenas
BUFFET CHINA HOUSE
2

# Acknowledgments

It's worth mentioning that this book was scripted and drawn through a tough year for many people. I was one of those fortunate enough to keep working, but many weren't. May we hear their stories as soon as possible. May better days follow.

*Twin Cities* came to life because of the efforts of many talented individuals. Editor Whitney Leopard and my agent, Elizabeth Bennet, were present from the initial proposal all the way through the printed page. Their input always made we wonder if I was telling the best version of the story I wanted to tell. In its final form, thanks to them, the answer is yes. We did it. *Twin Cities* happened because they believed in it from the beginning.

A special thank-you to Kristen Gish. Our mutual support makes our home a wonderful environment. During the creation of this book we both made big adjustments and came out stronger together. To my parents and siblings, I'd like to express tremendous gratitude. A lot of details regarding Mexicali, Calexico, school, and pop culture were inspired by conversations with them. Our upbringing was a source of inspiration. Even though this book is not autobiographical, it is rooted in the personal. Thank you for everything.

While I was growing up, I loved going to school to see friends. Quite a few of them are still important people in my life. Thank you for being there, whether to listen, shake your heads at me, or make helpful suggestions.

Huge thanks to Mabel Meneses for all the input on transborderism, which is a major element in this story. Transborder students cross the border every day to go to school, but "transborder" also applies to people who live in border regions and go back and forth for a number of reasons.

I wasn't aware this was a field of study, but thanks to Mabel and her recommended texts, I got to learn more about an experience I was already familiar with.

Before I started writing the script for *Twin Cities*, I talked with many twins. They shared stories about their favorite moments, tough feelings, and the events that marked their bond as well as their individuality. Thank you for sharing.

The schools that Teresa and Fernando attend are based on real private Catholic schools. The one in Mexicali is inspired by Instituto Felix de Jesus Rougier. Thank you to the principal and staff who allowed me to take photographs for reference.

Last but not least, something I found challenging for *Twin Cities* was how to approach coloring without repeating what I had done in previous comics. During the making of this book, I relied on the advice of my editor as well as peers. They listened to my ideas on color palettes for themes and gave me constructive suggestions. I'm very happy with the results. So to you, Orpheus Collar, Kel McDonald, Joss Martinez, and Bones Leopard: Thank you very much. It made all the difference.

# Notes on a Particular Word

Making comics that take place in Mexicali raised a difficult question for me: "Why am I writing this in English if it takes place in Mexico?" I understand the logic and have seen other artists and writers come up with great solutions. Still, it feels like a compromise. But since the dialogue and occasional caption box are in English, I take joy in inserting as many Spanish labels, signs, and interjections as I can. From changing the laughter of "Ha ha" to "Ja ja" to replacing a "Hey!" with an "Eits!" adding any indication that these characters are living in Mexico is an important element. They are small details, but I care deeply about them.

When I was writing *Twin Cities*, Whitney and I had conversations over certain words. The word that took the most attention was "pocho/pocha." For the record, it is pejorative. In this section, I'd like to talk a little bit about it.

I grew up hearing the word as a term for people of Mexican descent who lived in the United States and spoke Spanglish. At the time, Spanglish was not recognized as a formal language by most Mexicans or even Americans. There is also the word "pochismo(s)," which means to modify a word loaned from one language to another. In this case, specifically from English to Spanish or vice versa. For example, instead of saying "estacionar" (the verb "to park"), they will say "parkear," turning the verb "to park" into Spanish. For many on the Mexican side of the border, a "pocho" or "pocha" ("poche" didn't exist yet) was someone who spoke a mix of two languages and was not taking action to become fluent in Spanish. It was someone who, in their eyes, had abandoned their heritage and culture, starting with language. Like I said, it's pejorative, but some Mexican Americans have reclaimed and embraced the term. Some use it to informally mean they speak Spanglish and to signal their dualistic background.

So what's going on here? Is it offensive? Does it make room for a nuanced discussion? Why use it in this book? Like many things involving language and geopolitical circumstances, it has a long history.

First things first. Where does the word come from? It's a Spanish word typically used to describe fruit that is overripe, discolored, or rotten. So right away, it's not a flattering term.

Mexico and the United States are relatively young neighboring countries. Both have a history of colonization from European empires. One of the biggest marks left by those empires is the language. On the border regions, such a mark is vibrant. (I would like to recognize that there are indigenous languages still spoken in these areas, but I will stick to English and Spanish here, since I'm talking about just one word.) Living in this area can bring up difficult questions: What language does a person speak? English or Spanish? If you can speak or understand both, which one is preferred? Why the preference? Because, surely, if a person is proud to be from somewhere, that person must practice its customs. In this case, the custom is language. And what if that person doesn't practice such a custom? What does that imply about them? There aren't simple answers to these questions. They demand personal responsibility over something larger, with a long and violent history. There are many reasons why a person may not speak a language or choose to speak a different one. Calling someone "rotten" because they may not practice a custom is transgressive. It doesn't help anyone.

In *Twin Cities*, Alex is a complicated boy. He has gone through a lot, and his anger has gone unchecked. His bias says that if you're not living in Mexico or if you don't speak Spanish, you're not Mexican. Personally,

I don't agree, but his experience is one that many people can relate to. Moreover, a lot of people don't pause and unpack that bias. Meanwhile, Fernando is at a crossroads in his life and is influenced by Alex. Fernando has always seen himself as part of a duo, and now that his sister is seeking independence, he wants to cling to what he finds familiar—in his case, his Mexican roots. Teresa's interest in the United States feels to him as if she is abandoning her roots. Fernando speaks the term in anger. On the other hand, Teresa is trying to broaden her vocabulary. She and her friends speak a mix of Spanish and English. Their friendship overcomes language barriers, and as long as they understand each other, it doesn't matter which language is dominant. Still, the term is hurtful to Teresa because of how Fernando uses it.

Is it offensive to some people? Yes, absolutely. There are Mexican Americans who have chosen to embrace the term and use it with pride due to their multicultural heritage. That is a personal choice. There are many terms for people with Latin backgrounds living in the United States. Each of those are a mix of cultural history and choice. That said, from my own experience, I have always seen the term "pocho" as mean-spirited. Does it make room for a nuanced conversation? That depends on who is in the conversation and who's driving the discussion. There is always room for more listening.

Why use it at all? In this story, I decided to use it because it gets to one of the ongoing themes of the book. Two siblings are starting to grow apart, and in a heated argument, one goes for the meanest word he can think of. Siblings can be like that. They know each other so well, they know what would hurt the most. Within the story, I wanted to address that it is a word that intends to other someone. It was a big decision—I don't casually use the word, especially since both Spanish and English have a variety of wonderful words that emphasize our similarities and the positive aspects of our differences. To use it, even in fiction, meant being responsible for it.

# About the Creator

Jose Pimienta grew up in Mexicali, Mexico, listening to music, watching movies, and walking around as much as possible. They attended Savannah College of Art and Design, where they studied sequential art and developed an interest in storyboarding. After graduating, they moved to Los Angeles, where they currently reside. Jose makes comics with different writers and publishers and creates storyboards for films and commercials. Their first solo graphic novel, *Suncatcher,* came out in 2020. See more of their work at josepimienta.com.